BUMPIN' UGLIES

Episode 2 –
Date With The Prostate

Brandon Wilkinson
and S.E. Miller

By the same author

- Memoirs of the Messed Up Minds
- Me 1 Arthritis 0
- Beer Goggles
- The Tin Boy
- Dirty Dealer
- Bumpin' Uglies
  - Episode 1 – A Pain in the Ass

Introduction

The Bumpin' Uglies series is a work of fiction very loosely based on the Central Florida complex named The Villages, the largest gated retirement community in the United States. Over the years it gained the reputation of being quite the party place, stories emerging of sex, sensuality, and general shenanigans.

Around 2006 a Villages gynecologist rather controversially stated in an interview that she'd treated more cases of herpes and human papillomavirus at The Villages than she had during the time she'd practiced in Miami.

These types of reports tickled our creativity and Bumpin' Uglies was born.

Date With The Prostate is Episode 2 of 8 of the Bumpin' Uglies series, written in an entertaining script format by creators Brandon Wilkinson and S.E. Miller.

INT. FUNERAL PARLOR. DAY

Jack, Diego, and Marshall stand over Elvis's open casket. They're all dressed in black suits and ties with white shirts. About forty people fill the small room in the funeral home, with most of them sitting in the rows of seats starting about fifteen feet behind the open coffin.

MARSHALL
That's how I want to go. Kickin' the bucket while getting your leg over is a dream of mine.

JACK
So it should be. If that dream comes true you'll probably live until you're a hundred and fifty.

They try as hard as possible to suppress their laughter in light of where they are.

DIEGO
Marshall, *my* dream is to get you laid before I die.

Marshall ignores the teasing.

MARSHALL
I wonder what he was doing before his heart attack.

JACK
He was having sex with Yo-Yo Knickers. The police told us that already.

MARSHALL

I know, but I mean was he on top exerting a lot of
energy or just lying there with her bouncing on top
of him with those humongous breasts flapping about
his face.

DIEGO

Is that really important Marshall? He's dead
regardless.

MARSHALL

Yeah, but it would be good for me to know if there
are any particular positions I should avoid for health
purposes.

JACK

Marshall, worry about getting some action before
deciding what sections of the Kama Sutra you need
to avoid.

MARSHALL

I can't argue with that I suppose, but you can never
have too much knowledge.

DIEGO

Well you've more chance of too much knowledge
than too much sex.

JACK

Hey Marshall, maybe he was yanking himself while Yo-Yo was in the shower, you know, getting himself ready for the big event, and just croaked right there and then. If that was the case you'd better be very worried my friend.

DIEGO

Shouldn't we all then?

They all chuckle under their breath but quickly straighten their faces as Yo-Yo Knickers appears by their sides with tears in her eyes. She begins to speak but her eyes fill more and she begins to sob. Marshall quickly steps in and cuddles her, pulling her in close and looking over her shoulder at the guys and flashing them a wink. Yo-Yo Knickers finally gets herself together, pulling away from Marshall and wiping her eyes with a handkerchief.

MARSHALL

There, there, you'll be all right soon. He was a good man. I hadn't known him that long, but it doesn't take much time to figure out when someone is a genuine great guy.

YO-YO KNICKERS

Yes, he certainly was. I'm really going to miss him. Thanks for being nice Marshall, I really needed that. Anyway, I'm going to go take a seat. I think the priest will be starting the service shortly.

Yo-Yo exchanges pleasantries with Jack and Diego and goes off and takes a seat in the front row.

JACK

That was a bit strange.

DIEGO

How do you mean?

JACK

Maybe it's the skeptic in me but she seemed a little over the top.

MARSHALL

A guy just died in her bed. I'm sure she was crushed.

DIEGO

Come on, Elvis wasn't that heavy.

Jack and Diego exchange a high-five.

MARSHALL

And you guys say I'm inappropriate at times. There
was no need for that.

JACK

Maybe so, but we're getting away from my point.
They'd just met. It was their first date, and she
doesn't exactly strike me as the type that becomes
emotionally attached with the flick of a switch. Come
on she's a man-eater. She's probably had more
traffic inside her than the Holland Tunnel for God's
sake. I just don't think all is as it seems.

MARSHALL

Well I think we should give her the benefit of the
doubt.

JACK

I will. I just have my suspicions now that's all.

DIEGO

Marshall, you would give Jack the Ripper the benefit
of the doubt if he hugged you while wearing a tight
dress and sweet smelling perfume.

Marshall pulls a thoughtful face for a second before raising his eyebrows and nodding his head.

JACK

I hate to break-up the discussion, but the priest and funeral director just came into the room. Let's go grab a seat at the back.

They head off and take a seat in the back row, Jack giving Yo-Yo Knickers a distrustful stare as he passes.

INT. CLUBHOUSE. AFTERNOON

The clubhouse is packed for the after service get together. Everyone is dressed smartly in their black outfits. A long buffet table is set-up at the back of the room and the drinks are flowing. The crowd is mainly an elderly bunch, but scattered with a few in their thirties and forties and a sprinkling of kids; the younger ones bolting around the room like cars on a racetrack.

Jack, Diego, and Marshall are sitting at their usual table by the bar with a few of the other residents. Pam the bartender brings over a tray of drinks and dishes them out. Jack grabs his glass of whisky and stands up.

JACK

Here's to Elvis; a good man who'll always be fondly remembered.

The rest of the table stands and toasts to Elvis, chiming their glasses together.

DIEGO
It was a nice service. The priest did a good job. I didn't realize Elvis used to be an actual Elvis impersonator as his real job thirty years ago.

JACK
Yeah, I had no idea either. It was a nice service though, except the moment when Marshall dropped that fart and blamed me. I was mortified.

The scene flashes back to the boys sitting at the funeral service. Marshall rips a loud one. A stern-faced woman turns around with a look of disgust. Marshall points directly towards Jack and begins shaking his head. The scene flashes back to the table in the clubhouse.

MARSHALL
I couldn't help it.

JACK
Hold it in for fuck's sake.

MARSHALL

I had stomach pains though. I thought it was going to
be a silent one.

DIEGO
Silent! You nearly woke Elvis.

The entire table cracks up.

MARSHALL
It was a good one. In fact my stomach is still
churning, so if you don't mind I need to excuse
myself for a few minutes.

JACK
I'll come with you. I need to pee anyway. I want to
make sure I get that out of the way before you stink
the bathroom out.

Jack and Marshall head for the toilets.

MARSHALL
I don't know what's wrong with me. I don't think I
ate anything out of date or anything. I think I'm just
worried about Wednesday.

JACK
What's happening on Wednesday?

MARSHALL
A finger in the ass.

At the moment of these words they are passing by Yo-Yo Knickers who is standing talking with another woman. She has obviously heard Marshall's words as she has a look of alarm on her face and quickly averts her attention from the woman she's talking to and interrupts Jack and Marshall.

                    YO-YO KNICKERS
What did you just say Marshall? What exactly are you insinuating?

Jack and Marshall stop in their tracks, giving each other a look of extreme confusion.

                    MARSHALL
Huh?

                    YO-YO KNICKERS
What were you just talking about?

                    MARSHALL
I don't think that's any of your business.

                    YO-YO KNICKERS
It is if you were saying something about me.

                    MARSHALL
I was saying absolutely nothing about you. If you're really that nosy I was about to tell Jack about my prostate exam this coming week and that I wasn't looking forward to some guy poking around my anus.

Yo-Yo Knickers begins to blush.

YO-YO KNICKERS
Oh I'm sorry; I thought you were saying something about me.

JACK
Sounds like someone's a bit paranoid about something. I'll leave you guys to it, I really need to pee.

Jack leaves looking thoughtful and Marshall is left standing there.

YO-YO KNICKERS
I do apologize Marshall; I really didn't mean to be rude. I have a suggestion for you though. If you're worried about this exam with your doctor you could go and see a doctor friend of mine. She works at a local health center. I figure you might prefer a woman poking around back there. She's really attractive as well; a little Asian woman. I have her card here somewhere.

Yo-Yo Knickers goes into her handbag and finds the business card.

Give their place a call. I'll speak to her as well and let her know about you.

MARSHALL

Sounds great to me. I'll certainly give her office a call. I'm glad you poked your nose in now.

YO-YO KNICKERS

Look I really am sorry about that.

MARSHALL

Think nothing of it.

Marshall walks off staring at the business card with a huge grin on his face.

EXT. APARTMENT COMPLEX POOL. MORNING

Jack and Diego sit poolside drinking coffee and puffing on cigars. Jack wears shorts and t-shirt and Diego is decked out in nothing more than a pair of tight Speedos. Marshall wanders in dressed in finely pressed beige trousers and a blue short-sleeved shirt.

JACK

Jesus Marshall; you found some deaf, dumb, and blind woman with a poor sense of smell who's agreed to go on a breakfast date with you?

MARSHALL

Better than that Jack. Going for a prostate exam.

Jack and Diego quickly glance at each other, exchanging looks of shock.

DIEGO

Our doctor Tom Jenkins is slipping you a finger in the starfish and you're smiling like a chick in a Colgate commercial.

MARSHALL

Oh God no. No, I switched from Dr. Jenkins over to this other place. It's a health center that Yo-Yo Knickers recommended the day of Elvis's funeral. One of the doctors there is her friend and I have an appointment with her this morning. Apparently she's an attractive little Asian woman in her early forties.

JACK

It's not sounding so bad now. Those Asian women usually have tiny fingers as well, so that's got to help the procedure.

Jack and Diego again look at each other; this time exchanging appreciative nods.

MARSHALL

Exactly. There could be worse ways to spend a Wednesday morning.

DIEGO

Agreed Marshall, but you make it sound like a quick latex-covered finger in the pooper is going to lead to a happy ending. Female Asian doctor does not equate to Oriental massage girl.

MARSHALL
I know that. I might be an idiot at times but I'm not retarded. I was due for an ass exam anyway, so I'd rather have some hot foreign woman having a prod around than old Tom Jenkins.

JACK
Well good for you Marshall. It might be the most action you get for a while so I hope you have fun. What time is your appointment?

MARSHALL
Just over an hour from now. Figured I'd grab a quick coffee before I head off.

JACK
Do you think that's a good idea?

MARSHALL
What do you mean?

JACK

Well I don't know about you, but coffee goes through me like a race car driver and I don't just mean a numero uno. Put it this way, my first port of call after here is a date with the porcelain bowl. The last thing you need sitting in the waiting room is a few stomach rumbles. If you are actually expecting some satisfaction from your trip, do you really want the worry of dropping a log on this hot doctor on your mind?

Marshall perks up and looks thoughtful.

MARSHALL
Didn't think about that. On second thoughts I'll pass on a cup, but I did clean my back passage out pretty good in the bath this morning.

Diego spits out a mouthful of coffee.

DIEGO
Too much information my friend. Why don't you just head off now and maybe she'll see you early?

MARSHALL
Yeah, you might be right. You both up for a game of dominoes and a drink at the clubhouse tonight?

JACK
Yeah, we'll be there around seven-thirty.

MARSHALL

OK I'll give you all the juicy details then.

                    DIEGO
I can hardly wait!

Marshall heads off.

INT. DOCTOR'S WAITING ROOM. DAY

Marshall sits in the crowded waiting room flicking through an entertainment magazine, checking out the pictures of hot female celebrities. A short Asian woman with long dark hair and a white lab coat appears, holding a clipboard.

                 ASIAN WOMAN
Marshall Hunter.

She looks around the room. Marshall is smiling from ear to ear and gets up and follows her through to her office. He takes a seat and she goes behind her desk.

Well good morning Mr. Hunter, I'm doctor Chang. Are you Nancy's friend?

                   MARSHALL
That would be me.

                   DR. CHANG

She said she referred someone by the name of Marshall. I haven't met too many Marshall's in my time, so I figured it might be you.

                    MARSHALL
Well you won't meet another Marshall like me, that's for sure.

                    DR. CHANG
Nancy said that as well. So, you're here for your annual prostate check-up?

                    MARSHALL
That's correct.

                    DR. CHANG
OK Marshall, if you could go over to the exam table, drop your pants, and lean forwards over it I'll get things checked out for you.

Marshall scurries over to the exam table like a kid who's just spied a bowl of candy and drops his trousers and underwear, exposing his flabby ass. Latex snaps as Dr. Chang pulls on a glove and walks over to Marshall with a tube of lubricant in hand.

OK Marshall, just relax.

                    MARSHALL
That's easy for you to say.

Dr. Chang chuckles but continues on. Marshall is face-on with Dr. Chang positioned behind him. She smears lubricant on her index finger and the examination begins. Marshall's eyes close and a smile appears on his face as Dr. Chang prods around.

                    DR. CHANG
Well Marshall, everything seems to be in good working order.

Marshall turns to face her with bright red cheeks. Dr. Chang looks puzzled, but glances down to discover Marshall has an erection which is covered by the tails of his shirt.

                    MARSHALL
Really sorry about that, but it just snuck up on me without warning.

                    DR. CHANG
Don't be embarrassed Marshall, it's not the first time that someone has become aroused during one of these exams and I can guarantee you it will not be the last.

                    MARSHALL
Thanks for your understanding, but it doesn't make it any less mortifying.

                    DR. CHANG

It really is OK. Now, is there anything else I can do for you today?

                    MARSHALL
Well, I think my penis might taste funny.

                    DR. CHANG
Goodbye Marshall.

Marshall pulls up his pants and leaves.

INT. CLUBHOUSE. NIGHT

The room is fairly empty. Five guys including Jack, Diego, and Marshall are playing dominoes at the table by the bar. Pam the bartender is perched at her post listening to the guys rambling.

                    JACK
You actually got a full-on boner?

                    MARSHALL
I couldn't help it. The little guy just jumped to life. I tried to think about you guys, but Dr. Chang was really hot and kept creeping into my mind.

                    DIEGO
You were getting your butt fingered and you actually attempted to visualize me and Jack.

Pam from behind the bar roars with laughter, as does everyone other than Diego.

MARSHALL

I figured that would put an end to any chance of an erection.

DIEGO

Dude, that's so gay it should be pulling the moves to YMCA. There are a million things you could've thought about. What about baseball? I think baseball is the standard erection prevention thought process.

MARSHALL

Oh yeah, and that's not gay? Thinking about a bunch of guys in uniforms grasping big dildo-shaped bats and playing with balls.

Everyone other than Diego is now almost on the floor laughing.

JACK

He does bring up a very valid point Diego.

DIEGO

He does doesn't he! Never thought about it like that before. I am now, and will never use it again to keep the lead out of my pencil. But come on, thinking of us. I'm stuck for words. Think about farming or something then.

MARSHALL

But in some countries they're really into their
livestock. I heard that in Scotland the sheep can hear
a zipper coming down from fifty yards away. If I think
about farming I might think of those sheep, which
leads me back to thinking about humping, and
before you know it Mr. Happy is back at attention.

Diego just shakes his head.

JACK

Diego, I'd quit while you're behind. Anyway Marshall,
other than the stiffy, how was the examination?

MARSHALL

Well obviously it was good.

JACK

Wasn't sore at all?

MARSHALL

Not in the slightest. Plenty of lube and her fingers are
built like McDonald's French fries.

JACK

Nice.

MARSHALL

My only disappointment is that it's an annual exam
and not weekly.

JACK

You're too much. I'll tell you what though. I might get
her office number from you. I'm more up to date
with my car oil changes than prostate checks. I'm
well overdue for one, and like you I'd rather have her
giving me a finger insertion than old Dr. Jenkins.

MARSHALL

I would highly recommend it. Now if you find
yourself getting aroused during it I am absolutely fine
with you visualizing me.

JACK

Even if I was gay I would never think about you while
getting poked in the shitter, but I do have to say I
have no doubt it would put an end to any downstairs
pulse regardless of how much the hot doctor popped
back into my head.

MARSHALL

You're almost as much of a prick as I am Jack.

DIEGO

Hey, I'm overdue one as well. Maybe we can both go
and see this young hottie.

MARSHALL

Oh yeah, I'm the gay one! Coming from the guy
who's just asked another man to go with him for
some ass play.

Diego doesn't look amused but everyone else is.

JACK

Ignore him Diego; he's just looking for a reaction as usual. It's important at our age to keep the old prostate under control. Let's get her number and we can make a couple of appointments and see how good she really is. No harm in killing two birds with one stone.

EXT. YO-YO KNICKERS FRONT DOOR. AFTERNOON

YO-YO KNICKERS

Jack, you were the last person I was expecting. If I'd know you were coming over I would've made more of an effort.

Yo-Yo Knickers is dressed in gray sweatpants, plain white t-shirt, disheveled hair, and zero make-up.

JACK

Call it a business call, and you look fine. I always felt you slapped on too much of that war paint anyway. Well...let me rephrase that. You look fine other than the hair. Looks like you've been dragged through a hedge backwards.

They both share a giggle and Yo-Yo attempts to flatten it down with her hands.

                    YO-YO KNICKERS
Come in and grab a seat. Can I get you anything to
drink? Coffee, beer, perhaps something a little
stronger?

                         JACK
Got any Scotch?

                    YO-YO KNICKERS
I have Jameson's.

                         JACK
Perfect, close enough. Couple of ice cubes as well
please.

                    YO-YO KNICKERS
Coming right up. Mind if I have one with you?

                         JACK
Well, it's your house and your booze and you're
clearly over twenty-one, so yes I guess.

                    YO-YO KNICKERS
Always the smartass.

*Yo-Yo returns with two generous measures. Jack is
perched on the end of the sofa. Yo-Yo hands him a
glass and sits in the adjacent armchair.*

So what's on your mind, Jack?

JACK

Well, you've been acting a little weird in my opinion
since Elvis's funeral. The incident with Marshall and
myself the other day is a prime example. What really
happened with Elvis? No bullshit now.

YO-YO KNICKERS

Jesus Christ Jack, he died, in my bed for fuck's sake.
Why wouldn't I be acting a little weird?

JACK

Can you smell that?

Jack sniffs the air.

The stench of bullshit is overpowering. Marshall
mentioned something about a finger in the ass as we
passed you in the clubhouse and you would've
thought you'd overheard him saying you had a pussy
as roomy as a clown's pocket.

YO-YO KNICKERS

To this day I still do pelvic-floor exercises. I'm as tight
as a bull's asshole in fly season down there.

JACK

Nancy, can we get off the subject of your apparently impenetrable snatch and get back to the matter at hand. What *actually* happened? We all know you're pure filth. I'm pretty sure it was a complete accident, but for some reason I don't think Elvis's ticker just stopped during basic missionary. What did you do to get that heart really racing?

Yo-Yo Knickers head drops.

                    YO-YO KNICKERS
Okay, okay. I was playing with his asshole.

Jack, in mid swig spits whisky over the coffee table.

                           JACK
You were fingering his *butt* and he croaked?

                    YO-YO KNICKERS
Well, that's how things started. He was really enjoying it.

                           JACK
That's how it *started*. How the hell did it finish?

                    YO-YO KNICKERS
I guess I got a little experimental.

                           JACK
How little?

                    YO-YO KNICKERS
Strap-on.

                         JACK
Excuse me!

                    YO-YO KNICKERS
Dildo. Strap-on dildo.

                         JACK
Yes, I am aware of such equipment. You shoved that
up his ass?

                    YO-YO KNICKERS
It was well lubed after the prostate massage, but yes.

                         JACK
And that's what ended him?

                    YO-YO KNICKERS
Yes, but it was all completely consensual.

                         JACK
Well Nancy, I have to be honest, this wasn't what I
was expecting to hear.

                    YO-YO KNICKERS
What were you expecting?

                         JACK

Not that a man pushing seventy had a heart attack after taking a truncheon in the shitter.

                    YO-YO KNICKERS
Truncheon? It wasn't that long, it was only seven inches.

                        JACK
Only?

                    YO-YO KNICKERS
I have a bigger one. Wanted to break him in gently.

                        JACK
Nice. That obviously worked a treat. Great planning.

                    YO-YO KNICKERS
Come on Jack. Yes, I am a little kinky, always have been, but we were having a good time until the attack. Look, did our encounter lead to his death, yes, but it was probably just a matter of time. He obviously had some issues going on with his arteries that nobody – perhaps even himself – knew about.

                        JACK
That's actually a fair point.

                    YO-YO KNICKERS
Jack, please keep this to yourself.

                        JACK

Well, I can see why you didn't divulge all the details
to the police.

                    YO-YO KNICKERS
Jack, please just keep your mouth shut, it isn't going
to have any benefit if you don't. I never meant any
harm.

                        JACK
I don't know. Diego and Marshall are my best friends
in the world. How could I possibly keep this from
them?

                    YO-YO KNICKERS
I'll make it worth your while.

                        JACK
Go on.

                    YO-YO KNICKERS
Get your dick out and I'll blow you right here and
now.

                        JACK
You have to be fucking kidding me. You bang Elvis up
the pooper, the excitement causes cardiac arrest, he
kicks the bucket, and you expect that a quick blowjob
here in your living room is going to be enough for me
to shut my trap and never tell anyone?

Jack stands up and unzips his fly.

JACK (Voice Over)
Thank God for my morning Cialis!

INT. WAITING ROOM. MORNING

Jack and Diego sit in the crowded waiting room. The receptionist comes out.

FEMALE RECEPTIONIST
Diego Sanchez.

Diego holds up his hand tentatively like a nervous schoolboy.

DIEGO
That would be me.

FEMALE RECEPTIONIST
Hi Mr. Sanchez. Dr. Chang called in sick this morning, so you'll be seeing Dr. Lesley Velazquez instead. I just wanted to let you know ahead of time.

Diego is a little taken aback at first but quickly relaxes.

DIEGO
Oh, no problem. Thanks for the heads up.

The receptionist heads back through to the office area.

                    JACK
So much for French fry fingers.

                    DIEGO
I'm actually not that disappointed. I have a thing for Hispanic women. She must be with the name Velazquez, unless of course her husband is and she isn't, but I've got a good feeling. I don't even care if she takes two gloves sizes more than the Chang lady.

                    JACK
Yeah, I suppose. You're not as much of a tight ass as Marshall anyway.

They both chuckle.

A gorilla of a man of Latin descent appears through the door to the waiting room. He wears a white lab coat with a clipboard in hand that looks about the size of a cell phone.

            MAN IN WHITE LAB COAT
Diego Sanchez.

Diego again tentatively raises his hand. The man in the white lab coat comes over and extends his hand for a shake. Diego holds out his hand and it disappears into the clutches of the man's massive paw.

DIEGO

And you are?

MAN IN WHITE LAB COAT

Lesley Velazquez. Dr. Lesley Velazquez. I'm filling in for Dr. Chang today.

Diego, still in the hand grasp gives Jack a horrified look. We see a close-up view of Dr. Velazquez's colossal sausage fingers.

JACK

Good luck buddy. I'll see you back at the clubhouse

Jack bolts for the door and Diego is left there with the doctor, speechless and frozen to the spot.

THE END – Episode 2

www.ingramcontent.com/pod-product-compliance
Lightning Source LLC
Chambersburg PA
CBHW020521160726
47991CB00007B/3053